61	Alone
31	Do You Sleep?
80	Garden Of Delights
40	Hurricane
3	It's Over
74	Lisa Listen
45	Rose-Colored Times
53	Sandalwood
13	Snow Day
83	Stay
21	Taffy
67	Waiting For Wednesday
25	When All The Stars Were Falling

© 1996 Universal–MCA Music Publishing, a Division of Universal Studios, Inc.
All Rights Reserved

Any duplication, adaptation or arrangement of the compositions
contained in this collection requires the written consent of the Publisher.
No part of this book may be photocopied or reproduced in any way without permission.
Unauthorized uses are an infringement of the U.S. Copyright Act and are punishable by law.

Photo: Mark Seliger

SNOW DAY

Words and Music by
LISA LOEB

© 1995 Songs of Universal, Inc. and Furious Rose Music
All Rights Controlled and Administered by Songs of Universal, Inc.
All Rights Reserved

TAFFY

Words and Music by
LISA LOEB

© 1995 Songs of Universal, Inc. and Furious Rose Music
All Rights Controlled and Administered by Songs of Universal, Inc.
All Rights Reserved

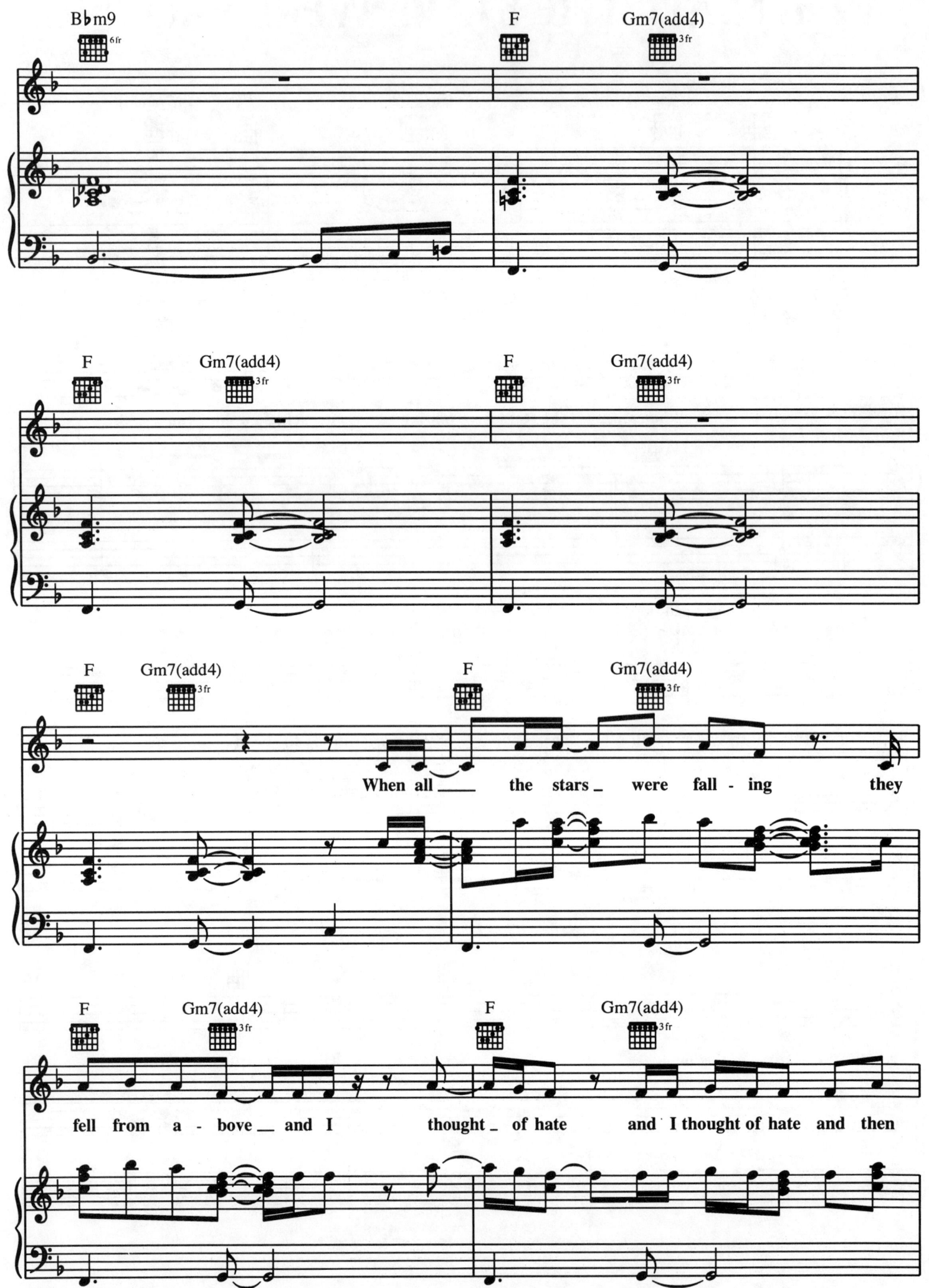

DO YOU SLEEP?

Words and Music by LISA LOEB

© 1995 Songs of Universal, Inc. and Furious Rose Music
All Rights Controlled and Administered by Songs of Universal, Inc.
All Rights Reserved

37

smoked with the ghost in the back of my ___ head. ___

Do you eat, sleep, do you breathe me an-y-more? Do you sleep, do you count sheep an-y-more?

Do you sleep an-y-more?

I don't know, ___ and

39

Lyrics: I don't care ___ if I ev-er will be ___ there, will be ___ there. ___

HURRICANE

Words and Music by
LISA LOEB

Moderately slow

Skel-e-ton boy by the side of the road, __ he warned me, he told __ me. __

He said, "There's this wom-an, she's a hur-ri-cane. She will heal your heart up. She is hur-ry-ing."

© 1995 Songs of Universal, Inc. and Furious Rose Music
All Rights Controlled and Administered by Songs of Universal, Inc.
All Rights Reserved

He said, "Don't look for hol-i-days.

Don't look, just run a-way. Go suf-fo-cate and choke your own cry.

Go where the wa-ter, where the wa-ter seeps from the pink sky.

But be-head this wom-an, she's a hur-ri-cane. She will

[Sheet music, page 42]

Chords: G F Am C G F

heal your heart up.   She is hur-ry-ing.   Re-

Chords: Em F

mem-ber your re-flec-tion in a pool, in a pud-dle."   And the

Chords: C F Em7 Fmaj7

leaves sped top-speed t'wards me   and my im-age was mud-dled.

Chord: C

"I'm a light-head-ed won - der,"__ she said.   "Don't you see my mind   slow down?__
"I've com-pas - sion for stran - gers,__   an af-fin-i-ty for dan - ger.   Won't you__

be my sac-ri-fice?"

I'm a light-head-ed won-der.
"I'm a light-head-ed won-der," she said.
Don't you see my mind slow down,
Don't you see my mind slow down

slow down?"

for you, for you?" You're a

head-less wom-an, you're a hur-ri-cane. You will heal your heart up? No, I will heal my own heart up, 'cause you are hurt-ing. I'm a sun-burst slap up-on your arm. I'll twist you till you break. You're a hur-ri-cane.

Repeat and Fade

ROSE-COLORED TIMES

Words and Music by
LISA LOEB

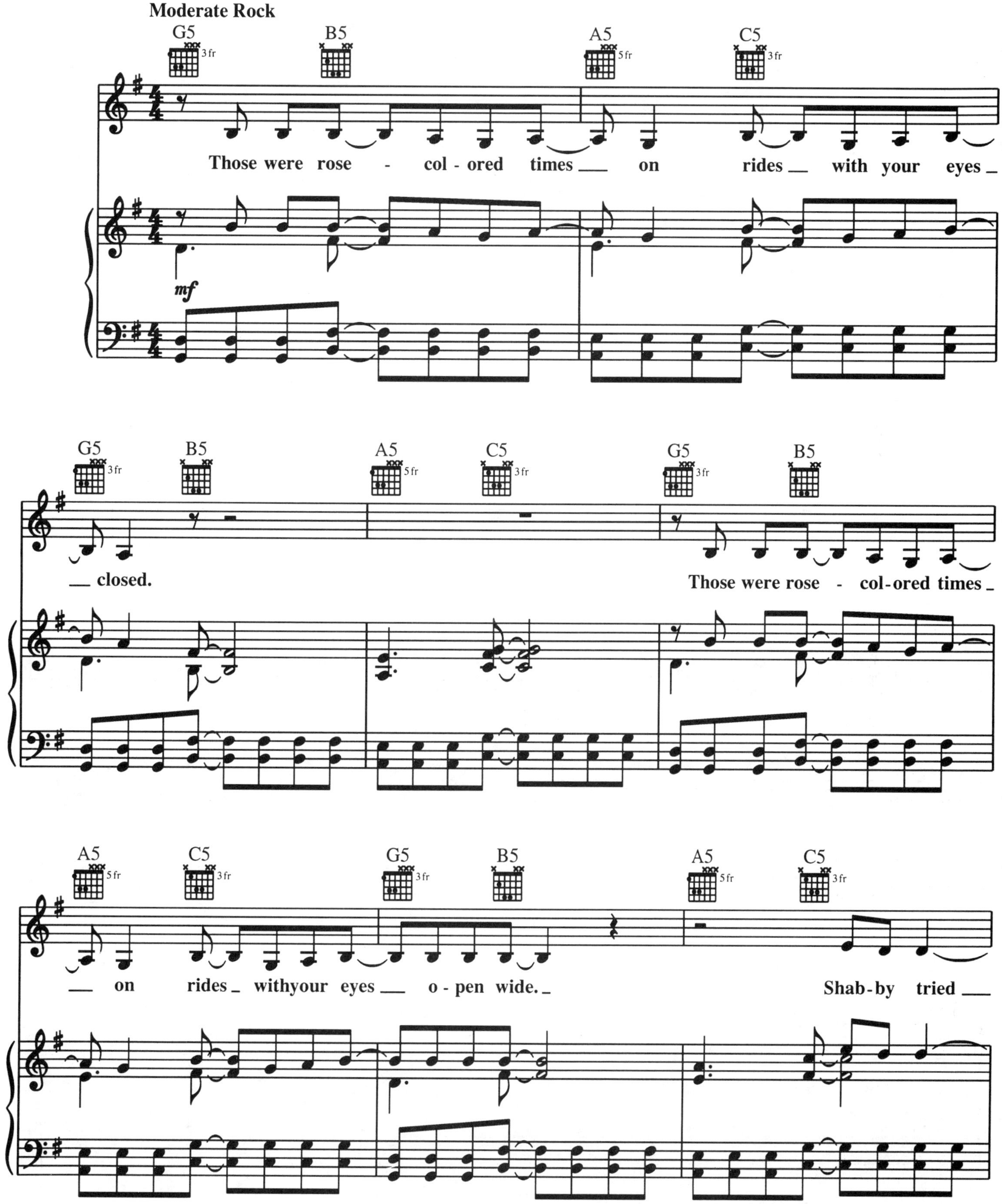

46

| G5 | B5 | A5 | C5 |

to comb her hair with the gift from her grand-ma. Her

| G5 | B5 | A5 | C5 |

blood tan-gled she got half-way.

| G5 | B5 | A5 | C5 |

Stick-y and pow-dered with dirt from the ground where her ma-

| G5 | B5 | A5 | C5 |

-ma had left her, had left

G/C
her,
G/B
had left
Em7/A
her.
C(add9)
G5
B5
A5
C5
Those were rose - col - ored times on rides with your eyes
G5
B5
A5
C5
closed.

Those were rose-colored times __ on rides __ with your eyes __ o-pen wide, __ with your eyes __ o-pen wide. __

Rust-y, the screen door, __ she o-pened it.

Raised from the ground. Ma-ma left __

49

Bed- I'll go with the man who looks like my father. The neigh-bors all tell me to go with him. He'd better take cau-tion, he'd better take care of me. 'Cause

Am7
C(add9)
if he don't he'd bet-ter be-ware of me.
G5
B5
A5
C5
3 fr
5 fr
Those were rose-col-ored times on rides with your eyes
closed.
Those were rose-col-ored times on rides with your eyes

o - pen wide, with your eyes o - pen wide, wide, wide, wide.

SANDALWOOD

Words and Music by
LISA LOEB

Moderately fast, in one

She can't tell me that all of the love songs have been writ-ten 'cause she's nev-er been in love with you be-fore.

© 1995 Songs of Universal, Inc. and Furious Rose Music
All Rights Controlled and Administered by Songs of Universal, Inc.
All Rights Reserved

Your skin smells love-ly, like san-dal-wood. Your hair falls soft, like an-i-mals. I'm tryn' to keep cool, _____ but ev-'ry-one likes ___ you.

Oh, I want to kiss ___ the back of your neck, _____ the top of your spine where your hair hits. And gnaw on your fin-ger-tips and fall a-sleep. I'll talk you to sleep.

But

57

C♯m7
4fr
E
Bsus
2fr
skin smells love - ly, like san - dal - wood.
Bsus2
7fr
C♯m7
4fr
E
Your hair falls soft
Bsus
2fr
Bsus2
7fr
C♯m7
4fr
like an - i - mals. And
E
Bsus
2fr
Bsus2
7fr
noth - ing else mat - ters to me.

A(add2)
C♯m7
4fr
E
And she can't
tell me that
Bsus
2fr
Bsus2
7fr
C♯m7
4fr
all of the love songs have been writ - ten, 'cause she's
E
Bsus
2fr
Bsus2
7fr
nev - er been in love with you be - fore, in

love with you _____ be-fore. _____

Your hand, so hot,

burns a hole _____ in my hand.

I want-ed to show you. _____

ALONE

Words and Music by
LISA LOEB

Moderately

I want to be by myself, sometimes I do. I don't want to be left behind, but sometimes I'm left by you. I pressed my tongue to the top of my mouth 'cause my jaw it was tired with the thinking. I

© 1995 Songs of Universal, Inc. and Furious Rose Music
All Rights Controlled and Administered by Songs of Universal, Inc.
All Rights Reserved

stretched my toes to the end of the couch 'cause my back, it was ach-ing from sleep-ing. So what is this weath-er and what is this dark-ness, and why do I feel so a-lone? When will it snow? It's been rain-ing for hours and why do I feel so a-lone? And when I'm left at home, when

you're with some-one else, I'm all a-lone. You do not cheat me of my child-hood, you bring me blan-kets for the walls of my forts. There is no an-ger with the eye-brows raised. When you do the fan-tas-tic I am a-mazed. So what is this weath-er and what is this dark-ness, why do I feel so a-lone? When will it snow? It's been rain-ing for hours and why do I feel so a-lone? ____ You were leav-ing some bar and you're com-in' down-town. You're not rip-ping out stitch-es, but you want me a-round, _ just to call you my love, _ just to call you my love. _ You are the treas-ure cus-to - di-an clean-ing the moon _ for me, scour-ing the sky so the stars would shine bright. You stand straight-faced and tip-toed on top of a lad-der and I, _

65

Lyrics:
I wait, and I, I wait, and I, I wait.

And when I'm left at home, I'm all a-lone, but I'd rath-er be a-lone with you.

Chords: Eb5 A5 Bb5 Eb5 A5 Bb5 | Eb5 A5 Bb5 Eb5 A5 Bb5 Eb5 A5 Bb5 | Eb5 A5 Bb5 Eb5 A5 Bb5 Bb Dm/Eb | Dm Eb Cm7 Bb F

What is this weath-er and what is this dark-ness, and why do I feel so a-lone?

When will it snow? It's been rain-ing for hours and why do I feel so a-lone? Oh,

why do I feel so a-lone?

WAITING FOR WEDNESDAY

Words and Music by
LISA LOEB

Waiting for Wednesday, my stomach doesn't hurt enough. Pain always is the sign.

Waiting for Wednesday, no proof of mine exists so

© 1995 Songs of Universal, Inc. and Furious Rose Music
All Rights Controlled and Administered by Songs of Universal, Inc.
All Rights Reserved

I don't have to take it back.

Don't want to show you good-bye, ____ show you good-bye, ____ show you good-bye, ____ show you good-bye. ____ But you're waiting for Wednes-day, ____ waiting for Wednes-day. ____

Em7 A D Em7 G
Wait-ing for Wednes - day, I pray you'll put me on the spot.
D G Em7 A
I do be - lieve you, that you'll love me, that you'll leave
Bm A Bm A Bm
me. Don't want to show you good - bye,
A G Bm9
show you good - bye. What will I do

when you come near to me? You'll put me on the spot.

You've been do-in' this a long, long time, not that you're better than me, but that you do it a lot. Now, I'm wait-ing for Wednes-day, wait-ing for Wednes-day,

D Em7 G D G
wait-ing for Wednes - day. I'm wait-ing for Wednes - day.
Em7 A Bm A Bm
I'm gon-na show you good-bye, show you good-bye,
A Bm A G
show you good - bye, show you good - bye. Now, I'm
D Em7 G
wait - ing for Wednes - day. You're back from out of town. The

West is dry, your mind is clear and I don't want to be here.

I don't want to be here. I don't want to be here.

to show you good-bye.

And I'm wait-ing for Wednes-day,
Lead vocal ad lib.

waiting for Wednesday, I'm waiting for Wednesday to show you goodbye. And I'm waiting for Wednesday to show you goodbye, to show you goodbye.

Play 3 times

LISA LISTEN

Words and Music by
LISA LOEB

Moderately, easy swing

Who would steal on Sundays? Who'd make them be-lieve, make be-
A sweet man will sing a sea-faring song.

lieve? Who'd buy a prayer when you can pray for free?
A dear strong wom-an cooes gent-ly a-long.

If the way you drank your cof-fee was the way you looked at me.
Good guys at the coz-y are ser-vin' folks for free.

© 1995 Songs of Universal, Inc. and Furious Rose Music
All Rights Controlled and Administered by Songs of Universal, Inc.
All Rights Reserved

G
Then I could take both my hands
D'you ev - er no - tice there's so man - y
off the T. V., oh.
peo - ple in bands in the ci - ty, oh.
Am
I've been
G/B
C
sleep - ing on half of my bed late - ly,
Am
and think - in' a - bout
G/B
C
what you said to me.
Am
You're tip - sy, you're turn - ing.

C
Em7
Fmaj7♭5
You are a - live, you are burn - ing, oh.
To Coda
Am
Li - sa,
C
Em
Am
won't you lis - ten?
The moon shines
C
Em
Am
for you.
You're tip - sy you're turn -

ing. You are a-live, you are burn - ing, oh.

D.S. al Coda

CODA

I will not judge you by the way you play your in-stru-ment. No, that's true as fic - tion, some-times I do. But the moon shines half - way ____ some - times, ___ too, oh. Li - sa ___

won't you lis - ten? ___ The moon shines ___

__ for you. You're tip - sy you're turn -

ing. You've got one foot on the floor. You're a - live, ___ you are burn -

ing, _____ oh, _____ woh. You al-ways wan-ted more. _____

Hoh woh, _____ woh. _____

GARDEN OF DELIGHTS

Words and Music by
LISA LOEB

Moderately fast Rock

I see the lights move on the ceiling.
You see the curtains draped in front of me.
I look right at your eyes, I look right through your eyes.
I see the lights move on the ceiling.

I see the stars up in the lights.
You see the sun come up alone.
I change conversation thought for you.
I see the stars up in the lights.

© 1995 Songs of Universal, Inc. and Furious Rose Music
All Rights Controlled and Administered by Songs of Universal, Inc.
All Rights Reserved

[D] [A]

I see the moon-beams on your fore-head, there. __ And I
You want to show __ me just what you can see. __ And
I throw a look __ that you can't catch from far be-hind. And
I see the moon-beams on your fore-head, there. __ And I

[G] [1.] [A] [D] To Coda

think a-bout the gar-den of de-lights. __
I, I turn a-way. __
you, you turn a-way. __
think a-bout the gar-den of de-lights. __

[2, 3.] [A] [D] [F#m] [A]

You see my face, you hate my
You are my Je-sus boy, you're

words, I hate you, too.
lay-ing on a bed-ly cross. You see my heart, it likes the
I've got you taped up to the

feel-ing that it gets when I'm with you.
wall. But real-ly, don't feel bad 'cause

you do to me all the things I do to you, I do to

you.

STAY

Words and Music by
LISA LOEB

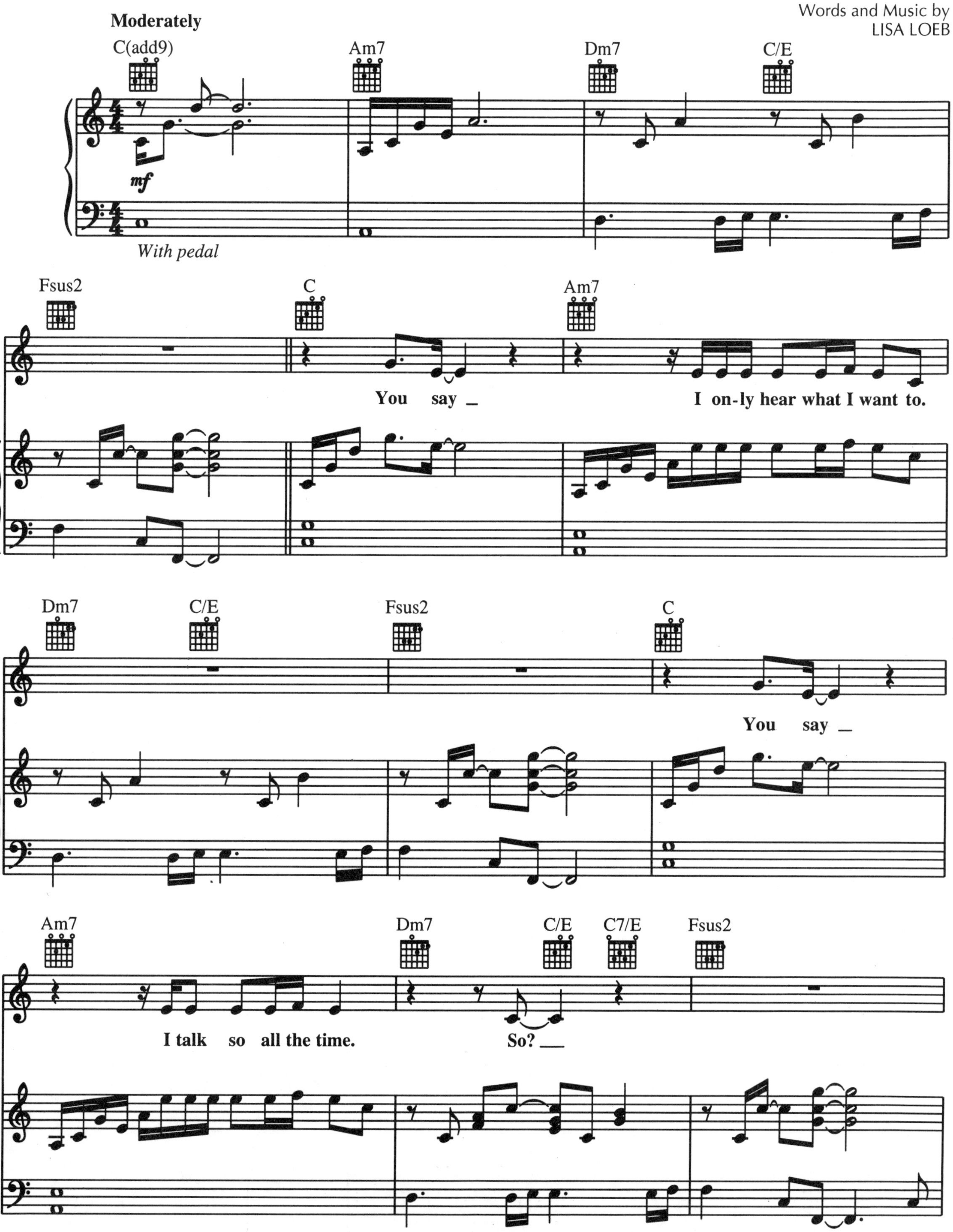

84

And I thought what I felt was sim-ple. And I thought that I don't be-long._ And now_ that I am_ leav-in'_ now I know that I did some-thing wrong. 'Cause I missed you, yeah,_ yeah, I missed you. And you say_ I on-ly hear what I want to. I

don't lis-ten hard, I don't pay at-ten-tion to the dis-tance that you're run-ning, or to an-y-one, an-y-where. I don't un-der-stand __ if you real-ly care. I'm on-ly hear-ing neg-a-tives, no, no, no. So I turned the ra-di-o on. __ I turned the ra-di-o up, __ and this wom-an was sing-in' my song. __ Lov-ers in love and the oth-ers run a-way. __ The lov-er is cry-in' 'cause the oth-er won't stay. Some of us hov-er when we weep for the oth-er who was dy-in' since the day they were born, well, this is not that. I think I am throw-in', but I'm thrown. And I thought I'd live for-ev-er, but now I'm not so sure. You try to tell me that I'm clev-er, but that won't take me an-y-how, or an-y-where with you.

87

| Fsus2 | Dm7 | C | Dm7 | C |

And you said that I was na-ive and I thought that I was strong.

| Dm7 | C | Dm7 | C |

I thought, "Hey, I can leave, I can leave, oh." But now I know that I was wrong 'cause I

| Fsus2 | Fm | Dm7 | C |

missed you, yeah, missed you.

| Dm7 | C | Dm7 |

You said you caught me 'cause you want me and one day you'll let me go. You try to give a-way a keep-er, or keep me 'cause you know you're just too scared to lose.

And you say, "Stay."

You say

I on-ly hear what I want to.